Something to Prove

PRAISE FOR *STORYSHARES*

"One of the brightest innovators and game-changers in the education industry."
– Forbes

"Your success in applying research-validated practices to promote literacy serves as a valuable model for other organizations seeking to create evidence-based literacy programs."
- Library of Congress

"We need powerful social and educational innovation, and Storyshares is breaking new ground. The organization addresses critical problems facing our students and teachers. I am excited about the strategies it brings to the collective work of making sure every student has an equal chance in life."
– Teach For America

"Around the world, this is one of the up-and-coming trailblazers changing the landscape of literacy and education."
- International Literacy Association

"It's the perfect idea. There's really nothing like this. I mean wow, this will be a wonderful experience for young people."   - Andrea Davis Pinkney, Executive Director, Scholastic

"Reading for meaning opens opportunities for a lifetime of learning. Providing emerging readers with engaging texts that are designed to offer both challenges and support for each individual will improve their lives for years to come. Storyshares is a wonderful start."
- David Rose, Co-founder of CAST & UDL

Something to Prove

Tiffany Jones

STORYSHARES

Story Share, Inc.
New York. Boston. Philadelphia

Published in the United States by Story Share, Inc.

Storyshares
Story Share, Inc.
24 N. Bryn Mawr Avenue #340
Bryn Mawr, PA 19010-3304
www.storyshares.org

Inspiring reading with a new kind of book.

Interest Level: Middle School
Grade Level Equivalent: 4.4

9781642611151

Book design by Storyshares

Printed in the United States of America

Storyshares Presents

1

She was not your typical circus clown. She spoke like a kindergarten teacher and her costume wasn't very flashy. Her naturally pale face was free of the expected oily paint. A small red paper heart was stuck to the end of her nose.

I smiled politely, even though I had never liked clowns very much.

"What's your name?" she asked.

I paused. I always paused. My pauses were legendary. "Derek," I said clearly. I was having a good day, and Sparkles seemed strange, but safe.

"It's nice to meet you Derek," she said, and her grin widened. She extended her hand and I shook it gently because it felt small and she was older.

"Nice to meet you too," I mumbled. This was getting awkward.

She dug around in the pocket of her smock and pulled out a roll of stickers. I couldn't see exactly what they had printed on them. "I just wanted to tell you that you are special. Did you know that?" She peeled a sticker off the roll as she spoke and pressed it to my shirt.

I knew I was special if special meant different, but in my case, different wasn't good. I turned back to the rack of clothes behind me and continued my search.

Thankfully, she moved on to her next custmer. I could hear her having pretty much the same conversation with an elderly man in the next aisle. Maybe everyone in the store was special according to Sparkles.

When I first arrived, I saw that the store was having a one-year anniversary event. Sparkles was the main attraction. A platter full of crumbs on a table up front led me to believe that there had also been refreshments. Pretty weird, but I was there for just one purpose: to find a suitable shirt to go job-hunting in.

I pulled out a blue polo and inspected it. No stains, no rips, and it was my size... the three musts for shopping at a thrift store. The tag said two dollars, which was about all my budget could handle. I could have asked my mom or dad for the money, and they gladly would have given it. My mom would have liked to take me shopping. But I wanted to handle this on my own.

In the dressing room, I saw the reflection of my sticker. It had a stupid little green frog on it and it said, 'I am special.'

I quickly pulled off my t-shirt and tried on the polo. I liked the color, and thought of how my mom would approve. She said royal blue looked good on me. I had to admit, it looked nice against my dark brown skin.

I had khakis at home to go with it, and dress shoes. My hair was cut neat and low so I would look the part of a professional. But would I sound the part?

I paid the cashier, a blonde girl that I had seen around school but didn't really know. I had just finished my junior year of high school. I thought maybe she was in a lower grade. She gave me my change and told me to have a nice day.

Sparkles waved at me from the dish section as I neared the door to leave. I nodded at the clown lady and headed back into the heat of the Georgia summer afternoon.

2

My dad told me that everyone has their own burdens, and mine is stuttering. At times it feels too heavy to carry, but mostly these days it is like my shadow... always there, but not always seen.

When I was younger it was so bad that I tried not to speak at all. Medication had helped some, but it made me feel like I was on another planet. I did speech therapy after that, and little by little it worked.

Still, nerves played a big part in my life. I needed to pause to arrange my words. These pauses were quiet on the outside but they felt noisy in my head. I was psyching myself out, though, because they almost always worked.

That summer I should have been driving, but I had waited too long to get my learner's permit. It would be another six months before I could get the real thing: my license.

What I needed even more was a job. I visited every business within three miles of my house and still couldn't get one. A week of precious, summer break was gone and my laundry bin was overflowing. Thinking of what my mom would say if she saw it like that was motivation to get off the couch.

At the bottom of the stinky pile was the t-shirt I had worn to Getzel's Thrift. The thrift store had been my first stop before starting my search. The sticker from Sparkles, now damp and creased, still clung to the fabric. I peeled it off and studied the goofy looking frog, wondering if maybe I had overlooked an opportunity.

A couple hours later, I pulled the polo out of the dryer and put myself together for a last-ditch attempt at employment.

The sky overhead was gray and the humidity fell over me like a wet blanket. Back at the store, the same girl was at the counter. She appeared to be sorting socks. Her hair was streaked with purple.

"It's my summer look," she said.

I didn't think she saw me staring and now I wasn't sure what to say. Glancing around, I saw that Getzel's was all but deserted.

"Cool," I managed.

"So are you as happy as I am that algebra with Mr. Fink is over?"

She had been in my third period algebra class?

I searched my mind and saw her, sitting at a desk in the back of the room. *Was her name Amy?* I thought it might be something like that.

After a pause, I tried to tell her I was very glad.

"I was w-w..."

It had been weeks since I had a block, but there it was.

"Wondering" had gotten the best of me.

"Are you hiring?" I asked quickly.

She stepped back and looked beneath the counter and I saw that she was wearing a pager. *Seriously?* I thought. *Who still had a pager?*

She handed me an application and a pen. "It's a possibility. Fill this out and I'll give it to the owner when she gets in this afternoon."

I filled it out right there at the counter and headed back home. I didn't have a job, but at least now I had a little bit of hope.

Something to Prove

3

I got the call from Pam Getzel herself the very next day. She wanted to know if I could come in for an interview that afternoon. It was a Saturday and my mom offered to drive me. "Good luck, baby," she said.

I watched her drive away and tried to calm my nerves. I wanted to save up for a car. I wanted to have my own pocket money. But more than anything, I wanted to get this job to prove to myself that I could. I needed to know that my stutter wasn't going to hold me back.

I pushed through the door with what I hoped looked like confidence.

"Well, hello there, Derek." It was Sparkles, but she introduced herself as Pam and I immediately relaxed. She seemed much more normal without the costume.

"Yes, I think we met when you were..." I began.

"Right, I was playing my other role," she said, and winked. She led me through the store and into the warehouse in back where the donations were received.

Through the open garage door I saw two older men outside smoking.

"That's Walter and Ben," she said, and the men nodded. "They handle the warehouse during drop-off hours and fix up some of the donated items too. Are you up for that?"

"Y-yes ma'am."

She didn't seem to notice my slip. Her voice continued, soft and steady, as we went back inside. "I'll also need you to help Ava at the register and keep the store tidy. She's my granddaughter, by the way. Her

Brother Andrew helps me some with the cleaning but he's..." she stopped and looked down. "He's not always available."

I was stunned, thinking she would only use me in the warehouse. I had no experience working in retail, but Sparkles was giving me a shot and it made my heart swell. I caught myself before I used her clown name aloud.

"If you give me the chance, I know I can do the job, Ms. Pam."

She nodded. "I know you can too, Derek. Ava says you're a good math student and that you stay out of trouble at school. I saw on your application you live close by. My husband Frank and I opened this store last year. A few months ago he suffered a stroke and still hasn't recovered."

I noticed the corners of her mouth turn down as she tried not to cry. "Can you start on Monday?" she asked quickly, attempting to smile.

"What time should I be here?" I asked.

"Come in at nine. Ava can show you around and then you can shadow her for the morning. I usually come in at noon, after home health takes over with Frank. Ava can probably answer any questions you have as well as I can."

I thanked her again, and promised one more time that I would do a great job. I hoped I was right.

4

I started walking home, dialing my mom as I went.

She picked me up after a few minutes and high-fived me when I told her the news.

"I knew you could do it," she said, tears shining in her eyes.

That was my mom. Sometimes she was over the top, but I knew she always had my back. My dad too, and when I told him the news that night, he patted my back hard.

"All right, son! That's my man!" he said.

In bed Sunday night, I couldn't hold my eyes closed. I told myself it was just a little summer job, no big deal, but my brain wasn't buying it. My friends would probably think it was pretty lame, but what did they know? They could spend their summer hanging out at the park or the mall if they wanted to. I planned on doing a little of that myself, but I had spent way too long laying low.

The next morning I was too full of adrenaline to be tired. I caught a ride with my dad and got to work fifteen minutes early, ready to prove to myself that I was bigger than my stutter.

Ava pulled up in an old pickup truck as I paced near the entrance. She unlocked the door and mumbled a good morning. She looked tired and I hoped she wasn't annoyed at having to train me.

"Thanks for putting in a good word for me," I said.

"No problem. My grandma really needed to hire another person, and I just told her the truth."

I noticed the pager again. "They must keep you pretty busy. Do you have to be on call?"

Ava looked confused and asked me why I would think that.

"Your pager," I said.

"That's an insulin pump. I have diabetes."

I apologized and she said not to worry about it. I felt stupid for asking, and my next thought was that Ava had a pretty big burden to carry, too.

Later that morning, Ava explained the sorting system in the warehouse. Our backs were turned when Andrew came in and his voice made me jump.

"Who are you?" he asked.

Ava jumped in before I could speak and I sensed she was on edge.

She gave Andrew all the basic information about me and my position at Getzel's, but offered nothing more. It was tense. I could tell right away that their relationship was strained.

Andrew looked like he was in his early twenties, and he looked rough. Something in his eyes made me feel uneasy.

He swept the floors and took out trash in silence, and Ava and I were quiet until he finally left.

"My brother," Ava began as we sat down for a break, "has his moments."

I waited, wondering what she meant.

"Keep your distance, Derek," she said finally.

"W-why?" I asked, my nerves causing trouble again. "Is he some kind of criminal?"

"No, he's not a criminal, he can just be really mean sometimes."

Ava was picking at a rip in her jeans and gave a loose thread a yank. She didn't say another word, just went to the bookshelf in the corner and started straightening up. I began to wonder if maybe this job at Getzel's was more than I could handle after all.

Something to Prove

5

"Derek, take a look at this!" Ava called from across the warehouse. I turned to see her wearing a gigantic sombrero.

"It looks great," I said, laughing and shaking my head. It had been three weeks since I started working at Getzel's. Pam was working the register while Ava and I sorted through a large donation in back.

It still amazed me what kinds of things people donated. Some things went right into the trash, like torn clothes or electronics that were broken beyond repair. Other items made me wonder if they were donated by mistake. Why would someone give away a perfect set of china? A handmade quilt?

We had been working for a couple hours when Pam came in. "You two go take a break," she said. "Walter will be here any minute. Oh, and bring me back a turkey melt," she added with a wink. "Please."

"Did you bring food today?" Ava asked me.

"Yeah," I said, "but a turkey melt sounds better."

"Let's go then."

There were a couple of fast food restaurants close by, but Ava had to be careful about what she ate. I got into her truck and we headed to the little deli a few blocks away. When she didn't bring food from home, it was her go-to place.

The truck we were in had been her grandpa's. It was loud and smelled of gasoline. Ava looked out of place in the driver's seat.

I had found out quite a bit about Ava over the past few weeks. She lived with her grandparents after she and Andrew moved from Pennsylvania just the year before. She said only that her mom had problems and she couldn't live with her anymore.

She'd been a diabetic since she was two, but the insulin pump was a new thing. Before that she had to give herself injections.

Andrew lived in a small apartment near the store that he shared with two other guys. He had dropped out of high school. In the years since, he'd done just enough to get by. I had seen him a few times and we kept our distance, hardly speakingat all.

The styrofoam containers squeaked together on the seat between us. Back at the store, we gave Pam her lunch and then walked out back. Ava and I sat down at the old wooden picnic table under the shade of an oak tree. It would have been perfect if it wasn't for the occasional ant trying to steal its tiny share.

I looked across at Ava, eating her grilled chicken salad. We had talked a little about my stuttering, though I rarely did it around her anymore. Ava had become a pretty cool friend. I knew I never would have been friends with her if it weren't for this job. It was crazy though, how I felt we clicked in a way I couldn't describe.

"I'm so glad I got this job," I told her, not for the first time. Now I wanted it to mean more.

"Me too."

"Your grandma is awesome," I said. "I mean, at first I thought the whole Sparkles thing was pretty crazy, but I don't know. She's not just acting nice, you know?"

It was true. Pam, much like her alter-ego, Sparkles, seemed to find the good in everyone and everything.

"Thanks. She loves everybody," Ava said and laughed. "But I know she can be intense."

We gathered up our trash and headed inside. Pam had us tag clothing and hang it on the racks, and then I helped Walter sand a wooden dining table. Afterwards, he painted on a clear finish and it looked like new.

That afternoon, Ava offered to give me a ride home and I gladly accepted. As she pulled away, I remembered I wasn't scheduled to work the next day.

I found myself almost dreading it.

6

"So how long have you been Sparkles, Ms. Pam?"

The store was quiet and Ava had the day off. Pam and I were working our way through the racks of clothes, straightening and organizing. I was just making small talk, but I had to admit that a part of me was a little curious.

"About fifteen years now," she said. "I got the idea when Ava was just a tiny thing. She was sick and the doctors were trying to figure out why. I'd gone up to be with her and her mom. My daughter was a wreck, already struggling with issues of her own. Ava had been admitted to the children's hospital for testing, and one of the nurses would dress up for the kids."

"Ava's face would just light up when she came in the door. That's what inspired me. I taught elementary school for almost thirty years. Being Sparkles is a way that I can make kids smile again, even big kids."

I couldn't help but smile then, too.

"I never could quite get through to Andrew though," she continued, but then quickly changed the subject.

"Speaking of Sparkles, I think we'll do a half-off sale to close out the summer. What do you think? We had such a great turnout for the anniversary sale."

"Sounds good to me," I said, almost getting tripped up on the word 'good' but dodging the bullet.

"All right, then. We'll start getting ready next week."

Back in the warehouse, I gathered up some items that were labeled trash and loaded them into a cardboard box. I could hardly see over the top. What happened next was so sudden that at first, I couldn't make sense of it.

There was a huge force against my back, and then I was face down in the grass, broken toys and junk everywhere. I touched my lip and there was blood on my fingertips.

"Don't you have enough friends already?" Andrew's voice was ugly and low. He had pushed me and now stood towering over me like an angry giant.

I knew I would stutter if I spoke, so I just hopped to my feet and balled my hands into fists. I was not going to be bullied by this loser. I knew enough about his type to know not to stay down when he knocked me down. It was a small gesture, but he did take a step back.

"Stay away from Ava," he said. "She doesn't need a friend like you. Next thing you'll be trying to date her or some crap. No way. Everybody else can be okay with black/white relationships or whatever, but that don't mean I have to be. That's my baby sister."

"Get the hell out of here," I growled.

Andrew walked away and I watched as he got smaller and smaller and then finally disappeared. He didnt drive, Ava had said, so I guess he walked home. I was just glad that he was gone.

Something to Prove

7

"Have you ever seen grass this green?" Ava asked me, days later.

We had eaten lunch and then walked over to the empty lot next door.

"It's very green," I agreed. I had told no one about the incident with Andrew the week before. I just explained away the small cut on my lip.

I thought Andrew may have some kind of mental problem, so I felt sorry enough for him that I kept what he did to myself. That, and I didn't want to cause any more family drama for Ava.

The sky was dark with impending rain, making everything appear more vibrant. The purple dye in Ava's hair looked even brighter, though I knew it had actually faded.

"There used to be a building here," she said.

"I know. I watched them tear it down. I remember when it was open. It was a Laundromat," I said.

She sat down in the grass, right in the center of the field, and I sat down so we were facing each other. I plucked a piece of the impossibly green grass from the ground and began picking it apart.

"I've lived in this town my entire life," I told her.

"I guess that's why you know so many people at school."

"Yeah," I said, "I guess." I ran on the track team and had known most of the guys since elementary school. The town wasn't tiny, but it was far from being a big city. I knew it must be hard for Ava, starting a new school so late. I didn't want to think of how bad it would be if I had to do the same.

"It's so weird," Ava said, her eyes focused on something far away, "that this spot where I'm sitting used to be a place."

"Well, it's still a place," I said, but I felt dumb right away because I knew what she meant.

"Yeah, it's just hard to imagine how so much can disappear."

I wanted to say something kind, something hopeful, but I couldn't seem to gather up the right words. That was how it was with me. I spent so much time trying to say as little as possible that when I wanted to talk, I was too out of practice. Later I would think of the perfect thing to say. And I'd be mad at myself, because it was too late.

I stood and offered her my hand and she pulled herself up.

"Thanks," she said, her voice a little brighter. "We better go get the box of letters and change out that sign."

"Right," I said, remembering that Pam had asked us to advertise the end of summer sale on the sign out front.

8

"Mr. Frank Getzel!"

I heard Ben shouting from where I was in the warehouse. As I came into the store, I saw a big man in a wheelchair. Ben had his hand on his shoulder and Sparkles was at his other side.

"Come here and meet my husband, Derek," she said.

Mr. Getzel's swords were a little slurred when he spoke, but I could still understand him.

"It's n-nice to meet you too, sir," I said. Introductions were always a trigger for my stuttering.

"Derek has been such a help around here, Frank," Sparkles said. "We're lucky to have him."

I told him that I was the lucky one.

The doors were set to open in less than fifteen minutes. A big plate of cookies and drinks had been set out, and 50% off everything signs were posted throughout the store. Many cars had appeared in the parking lot. One woman was already waiting at the door. Ava stood by the register eyeing the growing crowd.

By the time time Sparkles unlocked the door, a dozen people had gathered. The morning flew by and my stomach rumbled. Andrew was there, but he was pretty busy keeping the shelves organized. Since the incident, he seemed to have accepted that I was friends with Ava and that I wasn't afraid. But he still made me feel uncomfortable. And angry. How could it be that this guy was related to Ava?

I saw Ava grab her lunch bag and slip out back, but I knew it was way too busy for us to eat together. A little while later, the stream of customers slowed to a trickle. Ava still hadn't returned, so I grabbed my food and went outside, hoping to at least talk with her for a few minutes.

At first my brain didn't want to acknowledge what my eyes were seeing.

Ava lay crumpled next to the picnic table, her lunch bag sitting unzipped but otherwise untouched. I ran towards her and my stomach dropped when I saw her face. It was slick with sweat and drained of color. I placed my fingers on the side of her neck and felt the soft beating of her pulse. My own was hammering away as I leaned in to check for breathing. I felt the tickle of her breath on my cheek and finally the fog began to lift. I ran back into Getzel's, passing by my own lunch scattered in the dirt. I didn't even remember dropping it.

Once inside, I looked wildly around for Sparkles. She was in the children's section, twisting balloons into animal shapes. A small group of kids were watching her intently. She saw my face and I could tell it scared her.

"What is it, Derek?" she asked.

I felt like I was in quick sand. Nothing was coming out of my mouth. The half-finished, pink poodle fell slowly from Sparkles' hands onto the floor. The kids stared at me with big eyes and open mouths. I saw that Frank was slouched over in the wheelchair nearby, exhausted and now troubled. I knew if I tried to speak, a terrible noise would come out.

Except...except... Ava.

I only blocked on consonants, not vowels, and mostly on the first letter of words. Ava's name had never been a problem.

So I said her name and pointed towards the back. Sparkles knew and she moved quickly.

"I'll get her glucagon."

She returned with Ava's purse and groped inside before pulling out a plastic box. I ran ahead and knelt beside Ava. She looked worse than before. Sparkles was seconds behind me. She
fumbled with the box and managed to pull out some sort of syringe. She yanked down the waist of Ava's jeans and stuck the needle into her hip. She pushed the hair from

Ava's forehead and whispered for her to wake up. Everything was all wrong and I felt sick inside.

After what seemed like forever, Ava finally moved. Her eyes were slits and as soon as she sat up, she vomited. Sparkles and I helped her over to the bench.

"Are you okay, dear?" Sparkles asked.

When I heard Ava's faint reply, I felt weak with relief. Tears filled my eyes and I put my head down so no one would see. When I finally looked up, I saw that Andrew had appeared in the warehouse doorway. It was yards away but I thought that his face had softened, and he was sort of hugging himself.

When we stood to walk Ava inside, Andrew vanished into the dark doorway. By the time we made it inside, he was gone.

Something to Prove

9

Ava called it a 'low.' She said it had happened many times before, although that had been the first since getting the insulin pump. It was her body's reaction to her blood sugar dropping below a certain point. She was back at work the next day as if nothing had happened. But Pam brought in sugar free cupcakes and mine had the word hero written on it in blue icing.

"If you hadn't seen her when you did..." she managed to say before getting choked up.

I glanced at Ava and she looked a little embarrassed. The purple was a lavender ghost in her hair. Our senior year was just two weeks away. Pam had asked me to stay on part
time during the school year and I'd gladly agreed.

The extra cash was great, but there was much more to working at Getzel's than that.

"I was just helping a friend," I said.

Andrew was shifting on his feet, standing apart from the group as usual. "Thanks, Derek," he said quickly. It was almost comical how everyone stopped what they were doing to look at him.

I had already forgiven Andrew, but I was sure now that it had been the right choice. Standing my ground and staying true to myself had been enough.

My burden was still as much a part of me as ever, but something inside had shifted. I had learned that I was strong enough to carry it, and even strong enough to help others carry their own.

About The Author

Tiffany Jones lives in Central Florida with her husband and two daughters. Writing is her passion and she hopes to one day have one of her novels published. The Story Shares Contest gave her the opportunity to write a story that she hopes will be an inspiration to others.

About The Publisher

Story Shares is a nonprofit focused on supporting the millions of teens and adults who struggle with reading by creating a new shelf in the library specifically for them. The ever-growing collection features content that is compelling and culturally relevant for teens and adults, yet still readable at a range of lower reading levels.

Story Shares generates content by engaging deeply with writers, bringing together a community to create this new kind of book. With more intriguing and approachable stories to choose from, the teens and adults who have fallen behind are improving their skills and beginning to discover the joy of reading. For more information, visit storyshares.org.

Easy to Read. Hard to Put Down.

Something to Prove

www.ingramcontent.com/pod-product-compliance
Lightning Source LLC
Chambersburg PA
CBHW071226170626
46809CB00005BA/1962